PATCH
*Pachycephalosaurus*

TINA
*Triceratops*

TERRY
*Pterodactyl\**

*(\*a pterosaur
not a dinosaur)*

MIDGE
*Compsognathu*

PATTY
*Apatosaurus*

BRENDA
*Parasaurolophus*

In memory of Judith Kerr, who once had a tiger to tea. P.A.

For my niece Arianne.
This book was inspired by a herd of dinosaurs I drew for your 1st birthday! E.E.

First published 2020 by Walker Books Ltd, 87 Vauxhall Walk London SE11 5HJ • 10 9 8 7 6 5 4 3 2 1 • Text © 2020 Philip Ardagh • Illustrations © 2020 Elissa Elwick
The right of Philip Ardagh and Elissa Elwick to be identified as author and illustrator respectively of this work has been asserted by them in accordance with the Copyright,
Designs and Patents Act 1988 • This book has been typeset in Burbank • Printed in China • All rights reserved. No part of this book may be reproduced,
transmitted or stored in an information retrieval system in any form or by any means, graphic, electronic or mechanical, including photocopying, taping and recording,
without prior written permission from the publisher. • British Library Cataloguing in Publication Data: a catalogue record for this book is available from the British Library
ISBN 978-1-4063-6438-5 • www.walker.co.uk

# YOU CAN'T COUNT ON
# DINOSAURS!

## PHILIP ARDAGH
## ELISSA ELWICK

WALKER BOOKS
AND SUBSIDIARIES
LONDON · BOSTON · SYDNEY · AUCKLAND

# Let's count dinosaurs!

*Hi Rex!*
**ONE** dinosaur.
Yes, it's true!

Look! Here's another one!
That makes **TWO**.

*It's Rex AND Patty!*

**TWO** dinosaurs,
running round a tree.

**Along comes another one.**

That makes **THREE.**

Three dinosaurs...
Wait a minute! What happened to Brian?
Rex? Rex!

You didn't eat him
did you?
Oh NAUGHTY Rex!

So we're back to you
and Patty and just...
**TWO** dinosaurs, oh dear me!
Look who's coming!
That makes ...

**THREE**. *Look, Rex! Look, Patty!
It's your young friend Steggy!*

**THREE** dinosaurs on the forest floor.

Whoa! Here comes a MASSIVE one. That (finally!) makes **FOUR**.

*Now we have Rex, Patty, Steggy AND Argy!*

*Watch out, Argy, you silly-o-saurus!*

*Where were we?*
*Oh yes, Rex, Patty, young Steggy, and Argy.*

That makes **FOUR**.
**FOUR** dinosaurs off
to splash and dive! Here comes
yet **ANOTHER** one. That makes ...

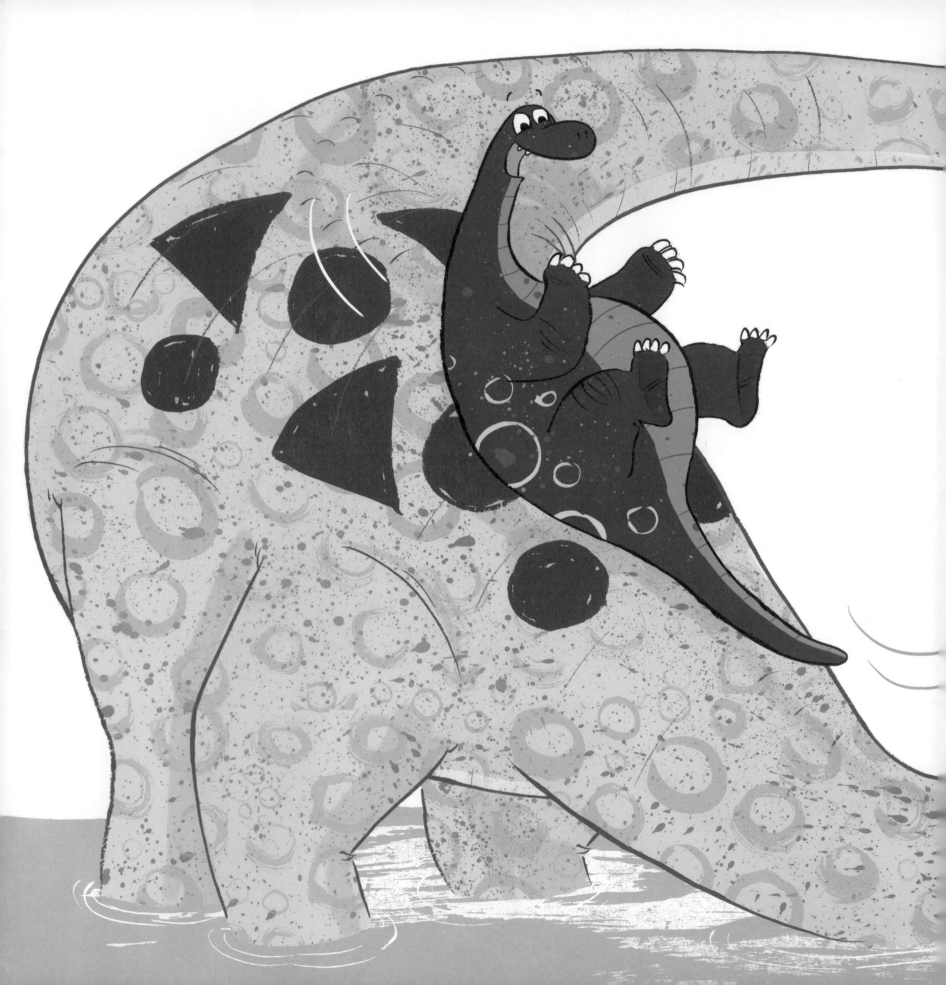

**FIVE!**

*Hello, Terry! Come to join*
*Rex, Flatty Patty, Steggy and Argy?*
*What's that, Terry? You don't count because*
*you're a pterosaur, not a dinosaur?*
*And dinosaurs can't fly? Rex can fly*
*and HE'S a dinosaur.*

Show us, Captain Rex.

See? He's very good at flying.

Now, let's count dinosaurs again.

Rex is **ONE**, then it's **TWO**, **THREE**, **FOUR**. Then it's **FIVE**, **SIX**, **SEVEN**, let's count some more.

1 2 3 4 5

**TEN!**

Ten happy dinosaurs all in a row,

Give them each a cheery wave.

Now it's time to—

*What do you mean one is missing?*

Let me count 1, 2, 3, 4, 5, 6, 7, 8, 9...
Rex? Rex!

Oh, I give up!
You just CAN'T count on dinosaurs!

ARGY
*Argentinosaurus*

VERNON
*Velociraptor*

BRIAN
*Ankylosaurus*

IGGY
*Iguanodon*

STEGGY
*Stegosaurus*

REX
*Tyrannosaurus rex*